JOJO LOST HER CONFIDENCE

CASSANDRA GAISFORD

DEDICATION

For my daughter Hannah—without whom this story would never have been created.
And for all the sensitive children and adults
I have counselled
You inspire me

1

Jojo lost her confidence.
She looked everywhere.
She looked under the bed.
She looked inside her head.

2

She looked under the trees.
    She even looked in the sea.
But it wasn't anywhere.
"Where is my confidence?" Jojo cried.

3

The great confidence bird in the sky soared high.

She swooped down and lifted Jojo onto her back.

"Who did you give your confidence to?" she sighed.

"I gave it to my friend," Jojo said.

"Why on earth did you do that? Confidence is yours. It's a treasure. Not a disposable gift," the yellow bird said.

"You must keep your confidence safe, not give it away."

4

———————

"What do you see now, Jojo?" The yellow bird asked as she flew with Jojo over the seas,
over the hills,
over the skies.
Jojo smiled.
"I see my sunrise."
"Can you see your colours shining bright?"
"Yes, I can," Jojo squealed.
"I can see spinning wheels of light. I can see all the colours of my chakras shining bright."

5

———

"I can see radiant reds and yummy yellows.

I can see outrageous oranges and glorious greens.

I can see brilliant blues and perfect purples.

I can see whizzing white light and galactic glittering gold."

And in that moment Jojo knew she needed the colours of the heavenly rainbow to be infused in her soul.

6

––––––

And Jojo took a deep gulp of air.
She inhaled the healing colours right there.
Down,
down,
down
Deep within her head, her heart, her body.
Then she blew
and she blew
and she blew. . .
Jojo blew those colours
through the air
and they floated up high and deep within like shining
bubbles.

"There is magic in me," Jojo giggled as they floated and fizzed and flew all around.

Plop! Plop! Plop!

They went as they fell to the ground.

She filled her aura with bright coloured light.

Jojo filled her body with happiness and joy and delight.

Plop! Plop! Plop!

She didn't want to stop.

8

———————

And then she felt it.
Her confidence came back.
In a beautiful, brilliant blaze of seven rainbows,
Seven butterflies,
and seven flying Unicorns.
And they said to Jojo.
"We were always here."
Jojo said, "Thank you for reminding me. My confidence is back."

* * * THE END * * *

AUTHOR'S NOTE

I wrote this for my daughter who messaged me in the wake of the Coronavirus pandemic.

"I've lost my confidence a little bit," Hannah Joy shared.

When we are stressed, anxious or overwhelmed our confidence can be one of the first things to be lost.

I made the story up on the spot to comfort her and allowed the story to speak through me as I left a message for her on WhatsApp.

Hannah Joy is nearly thirty, But confidence places no boundaries on age. I hope this story is a reminder to all of us that, no matter how old we are, what is truly ours can never be lost. Sometimes we just need help bringing back the light.

If you've lost your confidence, consider remembering all the things you love about yourself, or that others love about you. Write these down, and look at your list regularly.

Empower this awareness further, by recording affirmations and positive feedback in a digital app on your phone. Listen to these feel-good thoughts daily.

If you are reading this story to your child, encourage them to do the same.

Introduce an element of play. Go and blow some bubbles and surround yourself with gorgeous prisms of light.

Jojo Lost Her Confidence **is now available as an audio-book for your listening enjoyment. Check out a free sample or grab your copy from your favourite online retailer.**

ABOUT THE AUTHOR

CASSANDRA GAISFORD is best known as *The Queen of Uplifting Inspiration.*

She is a holistic therapist, award-winning artist, and #1 bestselling author. A corporate escapee, she now lives and works from her idyllic lifestyle property overlooking the Bay of Islands in New Zealand.

Cassandra's unique blend of business experience and qualifications (BCA, Dip Psych.), creative skills, and wellness and holistic training (Dip Counselling, Reiki Master Teacher) blends pragmatism and commercial savvy with rare and unique insight and out-of-the-box-thinking for anyone wanting to achieve an extraordinary life.

ALSO BY THE AUTHOR

Stories and Fairytales

The Little Princess

I Have to Grow

The Little Boy Who Cried

The Little Princess Can Fly

Where is Salvator Mundi?

Non-fiction Self-Empowerment Books

Mid-Life Career Rescue

How to Find Your Passion and Purpose

Bounce: Overcoming Adversity, Building Resilience and Finding Joy

Anxiety Rescue: How to Overcome Anxiety, Panic, and Stress and Reclaim Joy

Boost Your Self-Esteem and Confidence

No! Why 'No' is the New 'Yes'

More of Cassandra's practical and inspiring books on a range of life enhancing topics can be found on her website (www.cassandragaisford.com) and her author page at all good online bookstores.

ABOUT THE TRANSFORMATIONAL
SUPER KIDS SERIES

From the bestselling author of *The Little Princess* comes a brilliant new series, *Transformational Super Kids*.

These young heroes and heroines tackle modern-day problems with the passion and gusto of warriors.

They defeat cruel critics, they slay savage self-esteem demons, and they show people—jealous of their kindness, talent, and beauty—that their biggest superpower is staying true to themselves.

Suitable for 'kids' of all ages. After all, aren't we all still children at heart?

PRAISE FOR THE TRANSFORMATIONAL SUPERKIDS

"How beautiful. . ."

"Being released from the trauma …

This story is about the gaining of true power in growing into one's true self through childhood pain, discovering a new way of being, and knowing how where to go to gain help with being released from the trauma that had become one boys life. It is in the Author's Notes that this story transforms from a book to help children into a valuable resource for therapist and others who work with boys of all ages. Cassandra has captured a very typical aspect of how many boys are parented and the resulting chaos that becomes their adult-self. For those of us fortunate enough to have the privilege of working with men (boys of all ages) this sad yet beautiful story is one to keep handy and to share broadly.

~ Catherine Sloan, Counselor and Intuitive Therapist

"Such a powerful message…

Sadly beautiful and a real reflection of our current society, which if we are really honest has lost direction, particularly with regards family values. Training in family values is an absolute pre-requisite before change will occur. I took pleasure in finding out the boy who cried not only survived but was blessed following the day the tears stopped and he found contentment, grace, and peace. My prayer is we can only attempt to save many more such boys."

~ Kenn Butler, CEO

"A wonderful tool…
This book is a wonderful tool for anyone seeking to begin the journey to self-reflection and healing from difficult childhoods. Therapists will find this book useful for their patients young or old. To return as a child to discover where the source of the pain begins has always been valuable, but actually relating it to present day is key to understanding. Highly recommended."

~ Alma Hammond, Author

EXCERPT: I HAVE TO GROW

PRAISE FOR I HAVE TO GROW

"Courageous, compassionate and inspiring...
Courage is more than just standing up for yourself or doing hard things—it's doing so with compassion. Little Hannah is courageous, compassionate, talented and inspiring!"

~ Sheree Clarke, Midlife Courage Coach

"Such a powerful message....
This is a splendid little book for any person aspiring to reach another level, with such a powerful message. Of never, ever listening to anyone who steals your light. Cassandra is a shining example of turning every situation, including setbacks, into learning & growing opportunities.

As one who has taken advantage of the wisdom, knowledge & ability of Cassandra, to communicate, over a number of years, I would encourage you to read this book thoroughly & think deeply on your own situation.

For her daughter Hannah, with the voice of an angel & heart of God, you have indeed been blessed."

~ **Kenn Butler, CEO**

1
———————

Little Hannah was happily singing on her swing, when Little Angie went by.

"You think you can sing but you can't," she shouted.

Little Hannah stopped singing and ran inside.

2

"What's wrong?" Big Cassie asked as Little Hannah ran crying to her room.

"Little Angie is being mean to me," she sobbed. "She says I can't sing."

3

"Little Angie is just jealous!" Big Cassie told Little Hannah, giving her a cuddle.

"You have a beautiful voice. Promise me you'll always sing—no matter what."

DID YOU ENJOY THIS EXCERPT?

Sing Your Song! Heed the Call for Courage

Feeling discouraged, bullied, sabotaged or held back?

Part moral allegory and part spiritual biography, *I Have to Grow* is a timeless charm which tells the story of a young girl who leaves the security of playing small, to follow her heart and heal the world.

Little Hannah, is a beautiful and kind-hearted child, with a very special voice. When the cruel and jealous Angie tries to rob Little Hannah of her gifts she believes the answer is to stay small. But, things go from bad to worse.

Bullied and taunted Little Hannah doesn't stand much of a chance. Until a magical creature appears and encourages her to stand tall and shine like a star.

Liberate the music you have inside. Share your voice.

Life is about learning to follow your inner voice, live your truth and share your gifts. It is also about reclaiming your power, not hanging back, playing second best and being discouraged.

Find and cherish your unique abilities and raise your voice to the heavens.

Reconnect with your magnificent soul self and don't allow self-doubt or the envy of others to hold you back—you will reach your potential.

There are so many reasons why you should *follow your dreams*. **If you need some inspiration, look no further than this book.**

Be inspired by this journey to transformation and self-acceptance, and self-belief as our heroine learns to overcome the vagaries of child and adult behaviour. Her personal odyssey culminates in a voyage of self-belief, passion, and purpose.

From the best-selling author of *Mid-Life Career Rescue, Stress Less, How to Find Your Passion and Purpose,* and *The Little Princess*: a powerful, inspiring, and practical book about boosting resilience, overcoming obstacles, finding courage and moving forward after life's inevitable setbacks.

Find out who and what is sabotaging your success. Find and follow your passion and purpose faster.

Bonus: Free Excerpts from *The Little Princess*

and *How to Find Your Passion and Purpose*—overcome common obstacles to success easily (focus on your strengths, use anger constructively, follow your inspiration—and other clues.)

Available in Audio, Hardback, eBook and Paperback from all great online retailers.

COPYRIGHT

The intent of the author is only to offer information of a general nature to help you in your quest for emotional, physical, and spiritual well-being.

Any use of information in this book is at the reader's discretion and risk. Neither the author nor the publisher can be held responsible for any loss, claim or damage arising out of the use, or misuse, of the suggestions made, the failure to take medical advice or for any material on third party websites.

First published by Blue Giraffe Publishing 2020

ISBN PRINT: 978-1-99-002030-8
ISBN EBOOK: 978-1-99-002029-2
ISBN HARDCOVER: 978-1-99-002031-5